THE PROMISE

THE PROMISE

JACKIE FRENCH KOLLER

illustrated by
JACQUELINE ROGERS

A YEARLING BOOK

35 Years of Exceptional Reading

Yearling Books
Established 1966

Published by
Dell Yearling
an imprint of
Random House Children's Books
a division of Random House, Inc.
1540 Broadway
New York, New York 10036

Visit us on the Web! www.randomhouse.com/kids

Educators and librarians, for a variety of teaching tools, visit us at www.randomhouse.com/teachers

ISBN 0-440-41658-2

Reprinted by arrangement with Alfred A. Knopf, a division of Random House, Inc.

Printed in the United States of America

October 2001

10 9 8 7 6 5 4 3 2 1

CWO

For Sara, with love

CHAPTER ONE

It was the first Christmas after Ma died, and we were trying—Pa and Jamie and me—to make the best of it. Not that it would ever be the same. We knew it couldn't be the same, but the way I figured it, we had two choices. We could let Christmas make us sadder than we already were, or we could let it make us happier. I figured Ma would want us to be happier, and Pa and Jamie agreed, so we were trying. I was trying extra hard, both for Pa's sake and for Jamie's. Pa had been so silent and broody since Ma passed. I was hoping Christmas could brighten him up some. And Jamie...Jamie was only six and he really needed some Christmas magic to cheer him. Being ten myself, I was getting a mite suspicious about all that holiday hocus-pocus, but I didn't let on. I guess maybe I was needing some magic, too.

We were doing our best to carry on all of Ma's favorite traditions. Jamie and I made evergreen wreaths and a garland for the mantel. Pa took charge of the cooking. He wasn't so good at it, though. His suet cake smelled sort of like an old shoe, and the corn he popped for us to string came out looking more like coal nuggets than snow. But Jamie and I weren't about to complain. Truth is, I guess we were glad of something to laugh about. Even Pa joined in when we got done dyeing the candles with pokeberry.

"Lord, if we don't look like we've been butchered," he said with a chuckle. And sure enough, we did. We were so covered in pokeberry juice we looked like we'd been in a war—and lost. Those candles made a festive sight when we got them hung on our tree, though.

"It's a fine tree," I said as we stood back and admired our handiwork. "Ma would've been proud."

"Yeah," Jamie agreed. He threw himself down on the hearth rug beside Sara, our Labrador retriever, and stared up at the tree appreciatively. "I sure wish she could see it," he murmured.

"I'll wager she can," I said softly.

Pa didn't say anything. When I looked at him, his eyes had glazed over and I knew he'd gone deep inside himself to the empty place that Ma had left behind. I knew that

place well. I'd been there many times myself in the past few months. You can get lost in that place if someone doesn't grab on to you and hold tight.

I walked over and took Pa's hand between my two, then I leaned my head against his shoulder and waited silently until he came back. At last he looked down at me clear-eyed again and gave me a halfhearted smile.

"It's getting late, Matt," he said. "You and Jamie wash up, then go out and do the animals' Christmas. I'll get this mess cleaned up."

"Can't we stay up and do the animals' Christmas at midnight?" Jamie asked with a yawn. "I want to see if the animals talk, like Ma said."

"If the animals what?" asked Pa.

"You remember," I said, "the story Ma used to tell us?"

Pa still looked unsure.

"About how the animals all gathered around the manger on Christmas night and warmed baby Jesus with their breath," Jamie explained.

"And to thank them, God gave all the animals a miracle," I added. "Every year on the stroke of midnight, Christmas Eve, they can talk."

Pa nodded. "Yes," he said. "Now I remember. I liked that story."

"So we can stay up?" cried Jamie.

"No, you cannot stay up till midnight," said Pa. "You want Santa to find you awake and pass right over?"

"No-o-o," said Jamie with wide eyes. "I sure don't."

I frowned. "Then how are we ever gonna know for sure, Pa?" I asked.

"Know *what* for sure?" asked Pa.

"If the animals really talk," I said.

"Your ma said it, didn't she?" said Pa.

"Yeah…but…"

Pa handed me a towel and pointed to the water basin. "And what do you think your ma would tell you if she were here right now?" he asked me.

"I know!" Jamie piped up. He looked at me solemnly. "She'd say, 'Matthew, some things you just got to take on faith.'"

Pa smiled. "Exactly," he said. "And I reckon this is one of those things."

I gazed at Pa skeptically. "What about you, Pa?" I asked. "You believe it?"

Pa glanced at Jamie and back at me. Then he rubbed his eyes with both hands and heaved a tired sigh. "You boys are about wearing me out with all these questions," he said. "Go on, the two of you now, and tend to your chores."

7

That was Pa's way of saying *end of discussion, time to change the subject.* So I did.

"Will you play the fiddle for us when we get back?" I asked.

Pa shook his head. "I'm too tired, Matt," he said.

"You always play the fiddle on Christmas Eve," I reminded him.

He gave me a grudging smile. "You're not about to let go of a single thing, are you?" he asked.

"Nope," I said.

He sighed. "All right," he agreed. "I'll play."

"Lively," I said. "Not sad."

Pa nodded. "Lively it is," he said. "Now get—the two of you!"

Jamie and I washed up quickly, then pulled on our coats and boots. Sara bounded over to join us. She bumped my hand with her nose and sniffed hopefully at the sack of treats that rested on the floor by the door.

"No, girl," I told her. "You'll get your goodies tomorrow. These here are for the barn animals." She lowered her head and let her tail go all droopy, and Jamie and I laughed. "Don't worry," I told her. "Tomorrow's Christmas. You'll be gettin' turkey gizzards."

I lit a lantern and handed it to Jamie, then I threw the treat sack over my shoulder.

"Don't forget the suet," Pa called after us as we headed out the door. "Your ma wouldn't take it kindly if we forgot her birds."

CHAPTER TWO

We stopped by the smokehouse and I lifted Ma's suet sack down from its hook. Jamie and I had shaped the suet into balls earlier in the week, then we'd rolled the balls in seed, like Ma taught us. I slung the strap of the sack over my head and twisted it across my chest so the pouch rode comfortably on my hip. Then I hoisted the treat sack over my shoulder again.

"What should I carry?" asked Jamie.

Just the lantern, I was about to say, looking at his scrawny little arms. But then I remembered myself at his age, following behind Pa, always pestering to help. Everybody needs to feel useful, I guess.

"Here," I said, taking down a small string of dried fish. "You bring these for the cats."

Jamie beamed, then he leaned in close. "Can't I let Sara have just one?" he asked. Sara cocked her head at the sound of her name and wagged her tail eagerly.

I laughed. "Sure," I said, giving Jamie a wink. "But wait and give it to her while the cats are eating theirs. That way she won't feel left out."

Sara romped playfully around us on the way to the barn. She fetched a stick out of the woods and dropped it right in front of Jamie and me. Jamie picked it up and threw it for her, and she went bounding joyfully after it. Jamie and I laughed. It was good to see Sara acting like her old self again. She'd been so mopey since Ma died, lying on the hearth with her chin resting on a rung of Ma's empty chair, or walking round and round the house just sniffing, as if she'd misplaced Ma somehow and was determined to find her.

"Sure is getting cold," said Jamie. He blew out his breath and made a little white cloud.

"About time," I told him. "It's not natural the way it's been so warm. Just doesn't seem like Christmas with no snow on the ground."

We pushed the barn door open a crack and slipped inside. The air within was warm and moist and scented with the sweet-sour mix of animal smells and fresh hay. The cows stirred and mooed, and Bessie and Ned, our workhorses, stomped and blew us a welcome. Old Snoops, the barn cat, and her assorted sons and daughters came running from all corners.

"It's almost like they know why we're here," Jamie said wonderingly.

"Oh, they know," I told him. "Like Ma always said, animals know a lot more'n folks give them credit for."

We hung the lantern on its hook by the door, then I knelt down on the ground and opened the treat sack. I let Jamie portion out the dried fish to the cats and Sara while I went down through the stalls handing out apples to the cows and horses and ears of dried sweet corn to the pigs. When I was done, I pulled some lumps of sugar from my pocket and gave Ned and Bessie an extra treat. They neighed their appreciation.

"Merry Christmas to you, too," I told them.

Jamie came over and rubbed Bessie's nose. "You think it's true about them talking?" he asked.

I shrugged. "I dunno. I sure like to think so, though."

"Yeah," said Jamie. "Me, too." Then he

looked into Bessie's eyes. "What would you say to me if you could talk, Bessie?" he asked.

I tousled his hair and pretended to talk for Bessie. "I'd say, 'Well, aren't you the sorriest-looking little freckle-faced snip of a boy I ever laid eyes on,'" I told him.

Jamie grinned. "You would not," he said to Bessie. "You like me, don't you?"

Bessie shook her head and snorted, and we both laughed. Then Jamie stifled a big yawn.

"You go on back up to the house," I told him. "Sara and I can do the birds' tree."

"No, I want to come," said Jamie.

"Go on with you," I said, "or you'll be falling down asleep right here in the straw."

I had a special reason for sending Jamie on ahead. I'd hidden his Christmas present in the barn, and I didn't want him to see me fetch it.

"No, I won't, either," Jamie protested. "I'm just as awake as you."

"Now, don't be sassing me," I said, steering him out through the barn door. "I can see how you're yawning. Besides, it's awful late. Santa might be coming by any minute."

"You think so?" Jamie said with a little shiver in his voice.

"I do."

Jamie's eyes widened and he stared up at the sky. "Hey, look, Matt," he said suddenly. "Those look like snow clouds, don't they?"

I looked up at the heavy, dark clouds that were starting to roll across the face of the moon. "Sure enough, they do," I said. "Feels like snow, too."

Jamie grinned. "That'd mean a white Christmas," he said.

"It would."

"Ma always loved a white Christmas," said Jamie.

I grinned, too. "That she did."

"You think maybe Ma's got something to do with it?" Jamie asked. "You think maybe she asked God to send us a white Christmas?"

I looked up at the clouds again and felt a little shiver.

"Maybe so," I whispered. "Maybe so."

"I ought to tell Pa," said Jamie excitedly.

"You ought to," I said.

Jamie took off running across the yard, his little legs pumping to beat the band.

"Pa!" I heard him yell. "Pa, guess what!"

I looked up at the sky again. I didn't know if those clouds were going to pile up and amount to anything, but I sure wished they would. It'd be nice to have a white Christmas, and comforting to think that maybe Ma had a hand in it. I missed her something fierce.

CHAPTER THREE

I climbed up into the loft and dug Jamie's present out of the hay, then I stood and admired it for a moment. It was a little figure of Sara that I'd whittled from a piece of pine. It wasn't as good as the store-bought figurines I'd seen in town, but I thought it was pretty fine for homemade. The pale yellow wood was even the same color as her fur. I carried it down and knelt to show it to Sara.

"Whaddya think, girl?" I asked.

Sara sniffed at the little wooden dog, then licked my cheek as if to say, "Good job."

I grinned. "I can't wait to see Jamie's face when I give it to him," I said. "I wish morning would hurry up and come."

Sara wagged her tail and bumped me with her wet nose.

"I know," I said with a laugh. "It's not gonna come till I finish these chores and get to bed. Just let me wrap this up and we'll be going."

I found a little piece of hide and some twine. With my pocketknife I cut a length of twine, and wrapped and tied Jamie's present. Then I cut another ten or twelve lengths and put them into the suet sack on my hip.

"That ought to be enough," I told Sara as I took the lantern down and closed the door behind us. "C'mon, we're almost done."

An old logging trail ran right by the side of our cabin. A few years ago Pa had found a young fir tree growing just off to one side of it about fifty feet back from the house. He had widened the trail and cleared out around the tree so Ma could see it from our kitchen window. She loved to hang the kitchen scraps on the tree and watch the birds feeding. Suet balls, coated in seed, were a treat she saved to give them at Christmas.

I laid Jamie's gift down on one of the branches and sat the lantern on the ground. Then I took out one of the suet balls and commenced tying it on the tree. Sara sniffed at it hopefully.

"Sorry, girl," I said. "These aren't for you. You can lick up the crumbs, though."

Little bits of fat and seed fell off as I worked, and Sara gobbled them eagerly. She

watched me closely, tilting her head this way, then that, waiting for more. My fingers stiffened with the cold and I thought of Ma, working away out here all those Christmases past while the rest of us waited warm inside.

I looked over at our little cabin. It wasn't fancy, but it was cozy and comfortable. I could hear strains of lively fiddle music. Pa was playing already. I smiled to myself, remembering the feel of Ma whirling me and Jamie around the floor while Pa's bow flew over the fiddle strings. Firelight glowed golden through the kitchen window. I half expected to see Ma's silhouette appear, looking out for me the way she always did. It was hard to believe she wasn't ever going to look out for me again. Tears filled my eyes and I had to brush them away before I could go on.

"I sure am clumsy at this," I told Sara. "At this rate we'll be out here all night."

Sara suddenly gave out a sharp bark that made me jump. She lunged toward the house, and I looked up and saw a dark shadow standing between me and the window. At first I thought it was Pa, big and burly as he is, but then I realized the shadow was too bulky even for Pa. Besides, Sara wouldn't bark at Pa. Then the shadow grunted and all the hairs on my head stood up.

A bear!

CHAPTER FOUR

"No, Sara, no!" I cried. Sara was big-boned and powerful, but I knew she wasn't no match for a bear. "Come!" I commanded loudly. "Sara! You *come*, y'hear?"

Sara gave a few more warning barks, then reluctantly returned to my side. I grabbed her collar and held on tight. The bear stood on its hind legs, eyeing us curiously. It was a big, fat one and should've been hibernating. I figured the warm spell must've woken it up, but chances were it was pretty sleepy. I looked beyond it, at the house, trying to figure a way to get past it to safety. The bear stood square in the middle of the trail, though, and the woods on either side were a tangle of briers and underbrush.

Sara growled low in her throat. Her head was down and the hair on her back stood up on end.

"Easy, girl," I told her. "If we just stay still, maybe it'll go back the way it came."

The bear sniffed the air and gave out another grunt. Then it dropped to all fours.

Sara broke free of my grip and lunged. She charged across the clearing and challenged the bear again, growling and snarling in its face.

"Sara! Get back here *now*!" I shouted, but Sara paid no heed. The bear eyed her stupidly for a while, just swaying slowly side to side as if wondering what to make of her.

She charged in close, and the bear tossed its head and growled low and threateningly.

"Sara, come back!" I shouted again.

Sara trotted back to me at last, but it was too late. She'd gone and got the bear all riled up. It was loping across the clearing straight toward us!

"Pa!" I shouted toward the house. "Pa!"

The fiddle played on, sprightly and loud. There was no way Pa would hear. I hesitated a moment, thinking maybe I could keep the tree between me and the bear, circling around it until I could make a dash for the house. But the tree was awful small, and the bear was awful big. And the closer it got, the bigger it looked! At the last moment I panicked and started to run, racing down the old logging trail, away from the house, toward the piney woods.

Sara ran with me, but she kept dropping

back every few minutes to challenge the bear again. I was grateful for that because she slowed it down some, but I worried what it might do to her if it caught her.

As I ran, I tried to plan out what to do. I wanted to circle back to the house, but even if I could find my way through the briers, the land down here was low and swampy. Normally it would be frozen this time of year, but with the warm spell we'd been having I couldn't take the chance. If I got bogged down in the swamp, the bear would be on me in no time. I could try to hide or climb a tree, but bears can follow a scent like a hound dog and they can climb trees, too. And dogs can't. I knew Sara'd stand and fight if the bear got too close. I had to keep running and hope that Pa missed me before long.

The bear kept coming on at a steady pace.

It seemed determined, but not in any great hurry. I knew it could have run me down if it really wanted to. A bear can run a man down easy. I kept praying I would come to a hill. Pa always told me to run downhill if a bear was chasing me because that's the only time a man has the advantage. I reached the piney woods and kept right on going until I came out the other side. I'd never been so far along the logging trail before. It twisted and turned so that soon I had no sense of what direction I was headed. I looked back, hoping to see some sign of Pa, but all I could see was Sara and the bear.

I was tuckered and getting panicky. My legs ached from running in my heavy boots and my breath came out in ragged puffs. I had to get away from that bear or I was finished. At last the trail came out on a ridge, and the land fell away on either side. The woods were thick and the terrain pitched sharply, and the way I saw it I had no choice. I struck off the trail and plunged down the hill. It was hard going, but I had to put some distance between me and that bear. With any luck it would get discouraged and give up the chase.

Branches snagged at my clothes and whipped across my face as I half ran, half stumbled down the steep hillside. Sara scooted through the underbrush ahead of me. She'd given off worrying the bear for the time being and seemed more intent on scouting out a path for me to follow. I looked back. The bear was no longer in sight, but heavy crashing sounds told me it was still on our trail.

Sara led the way down and down, and I scrambled after her. After a while, the hillside flattened out and I stumbled on, first this way, then that, wherever I could find a break in the underbrush. The bear appeared behind us again, and Sara dropped back and started worrying at it once more. My breath was coming out in big gasps and my lungs felt near to bursting. I didn't know how much longer I could keep picking my feet up and putting them down. I tripped and fell, then scrambled to my feet, staggered on a little further, and fell again. It was no use. I couldn't go on. A big pine tree loomed up in front of me and I did the only thing left to do. I climbed it.

CHAPTER FIVE

I clung to the trunk, my chest heaving and my heart pounding. I shouted at Sara as she took up her post beneath me.

"No, Sara," I called. "Run, girl! Run away!"

But I knew she wouldn't leave.

There was a shuffling and crashing, and then the bear was there, just a few feet away. Sara set up a frenzied barking and began to charge. She flew at the bear's face, trying to get close to its neck, then she darted back and dashed in again from a different angle.

The bear tolerated her for a while, turning away from her attacks as if she were no more than an annoying flea. But then one of Sara's lunges hit home. She sank her teeth into the bear's left shoulder. With a roar of indignant rage it reared up and shook her loose. It had finally had enough. The bear dropped down again and charged Sara. She was faster, though. Like lightning, she whipped around and came at it from behind.

"That's it, girl!" I cried. "Just keep out of the way of those claws!"

Sara snapped at the bear's right flank, and it whirled, but she was too fast once again. She dropped back and circled, ears flat and lips curled. The bear circled, too, keeping a wary eye on her.

I began to feel a glimmer of hope. If Sara could just keep at the bear until it tired, maybe it would give up and go away.

"Good girl, Sara!" I cried. "Just take your time."

Suddenly Sara charged in again, snapping and growling. She lashed at the bear's right front leg and the bear reared up and flailed at her. I sucked in a sharp breath as the great paw grazed her back. Before I could holler for her to watch out, Sara whirled in midair and swooped in once again, aiming for the bear's belly. This time the bear was ready, though. With one great paw it caught her under the chest and hefted her high into the air. There was a yelp, a thud, and then silence.

"Sara?" I croaked.

The bear paused a moment, then dropped to all fours and lumbered over to Sara's still body.

"No!" I cried. "Leave her alone!"

The bear paid me no mind. It swung its head in the air over Sara, then sniffed, lifted its nose, and turned toward me. I flattened myself against the trunk, hoping it wouldn't see me in the dark. It had no trouble locating me, though. It shuffled over to the tree and looked straight up at me, its beady black eyes glinting in the moonlight. Then it reared up, grabbed the tree, and started to shake. The tree trembled and so did I, but I just clung all the tighter. There was no way that bear was gonna shake me out, and I guess it knew that 'cause next thing it grabbed the trunk with all four paws and started to climb.

I climbed, too, with my heart pounding. Higher and higher I went, prickly old branches snagging at me and tearing at my clothes. At last the stub of a broken branch snagged my coat and held me fast. I yanked and yanked at the coat and then I looked down and saw that it wasn't my coat that was snagged at all. It was the suet sack. In my panic I'd forgotten I still had it strapped around my chest. The bear sniffed the air again and suddenly I realized what it was after. It didn't want me. It wanted the suet!

I yanked the strap up over my head and lowered the sack down near the bear's snout so it could get a good whiff. Then I hauled off and flung the sack as far and as hard as I could. It crashed into the brush some distance away. The bear turned its head toward the sound, sniffed, then backed down the trunk and loped off.

I watched as the bear poked at the sack with its snout. With a satisfied grunt, it picked the sack up and ambled off. In a rush of relief, I collapsed against the trunk, trembly and weak. I closed my eyes to rest for a minute, and then I heard a faint whimper.

"Sara!" My eyes flew open again. I was so plumb tired I'd forgotten about Sara. I scrambled down from the tree and rushed over to where she lay. She was on her side, her neck and chest red with blood.

"Sara?" I called softly.

Her tail thumped feebly and she tried to raise her head, but her eyes were glazed with pain. I dropped to my knees.

"You okay, girl?" I asked. "Can you get up?"

She tried once more to lift her head, then whimpered and lay still. I looked more closely at her wounds. They were deep and bleeding hard.

"Oh, Sara," I whispered.

I pulled off my coat and wrapped it around her as best I could. She cried pitifully each time I touched her.

"You'll be okay, girl," I said, tears blurring my sight. "I just got to figure a way to get you home. That's all."

I couldn't carry her. I knew that. She weighed near as much as me. I might have been able to make a travois, but could I pull it up that steep hill we'd come down? I looked around, shivering in my shirt. Which hill was it, anyway? We were down in some valley now, and there were hills all around us. My heart sank. I didn't even know where we were, let alone how to get us home.

Sara whimpered once more, faintly.

I put my face down close to hers.

"You just hang on now, y'hear?" I said. "Pa's bound to be out looking for us. He'll find us soon enough."

I stood and cupped my hands around my mouth.

"Pa!" I shouted. "Pa! Can you hear me?"

I listened to my own voice echoing off into the wilderness. I strained to hear a reply, but I heard nothing…nothing but the rustling of wind in the trees.

CHAPTER SIX

The night grew colder and darker as the wind picked up and more and more clouds rolled in. I yelled until my voice was hoarse, then I lay down next to Sara for warmth. She hadn't made any noise in some time, but I could feel her still breathing. I hoped she was just sleeping. After a while I guess I drifted off, too.

"Matt. Matthew, wake up!"

I sat up quick and looked around. It was a soft female voice. It sounded like…Ma! But Ma was…

"Matt," the voice called again.

I looked up at the sky.

"Ma?" I said.

"Here, Matt."

I looked down again. The voice was coming from right in front of me. From...no. It couldn't be. Sara's eyes were open, her head was up, and she was looking at me.

"Sara?" I said.

The voice came again. "You've got to go for help," it said.

I shook my head. Was I hearing things? Sara's mouth wasn't moving or anything, but the voice seemed to be coming straight from her. And there was something strange in her eyes, too. Something like *knowing*.

A shiver ran through me. It *was* Christmas Eve. And, I reckoned, pretty close to midnight.

I stared at Sara again. "Are you...talking?" I asked.

Sara's eyes looked clearly into mine. "Snow's coming," said the voice, softly but urgently. "You've got to go for help."

She *was* talking! She had to be. But why was she trying to send me away?

"I can't leave you," I said. "What if something happens? What if…"

"Nothing will happen," said the voice.

"How do you know?" I asked.

"I know."

"You'll be here, alive, when I get back? You promise?"

"I promise."

"But…" I looked around. "I don't know the way."

"Keep the North Star off your left shoulder."

I looked up. The clouds were rolling by, but I could still glimpse the stars through the breaks.

"Go quickly," said the voice. It was growing

fainter. Then Sara closed her eyes and her head drooped again.

"Sara?" I whispered.

She made no move, no sound. I looked all around again. Had she really spoken, or…I looked up at the sky. Or was it Ma? Or was it just my imagination, running wild?

There was no answer. Nothing but the rush of wind.

Sara whimpered softly, urgently, and I remembered Ma's favorite saying, the one Jamie had reminded me of just that evening. *Some things you just got to take on faith.*

"All right," I said, blinking back tears. I knelt and gave Sara a hug. "I'm going, like you said. But you hang on. You be here when I get back, like you promised."

I rose and turned so that the North Star was off my left shoulder and I started to run.

CHAPTER SEVEN

The wind wailed in my ears. It numbed my face and stung my eyes until they watered. Clouds raced by, making it hard to keep a fix on the star. Nothing looked familiar. I had no way of telling if I was heading toward home or away, no way but the words of...what? A dog? An angel? Or a dream?

Faith, I reminded myself. *You got to have faith.*

I reached a steep hillside and started to climb. The star was hidden by the thickening clouds, and snowflakes were beginning to fall. Now what? I wondered. What do I do now? Up and up I went, and at last, at the top, I came upon the old logging trail!

But which way was home? I'd gotten so turned around in my head I didn't know what direction I was facing. I looked for the star again. "Please. Just a glimpse," I whispered. But all I could see was snow, hurling at me out of the darkness.

"Sara," I whispered. "Or Ma. If either of you can hear me, please tell me what to do."

Then I listened real close and hard for an answer. And then I heard it—faint and far away. Pa's voice, calling my name!

My heart leapt.

"Pa!" I cried. "Pa!" But the wind blew my

words right back into my mouth. I knew Pa wouldn't hear me. I listened till I heard him call again so I could get a fix on his voice. Then I took off running.

The snow fell heavily and the wind tore at my thin shirt with icy claws. All I could think of was Sara, lying back there in the valley, hurt and cold and alone.

"You hang on," I whispered fiercely. "You hang on, like you promised."

Pa's voice was growing louder. And I heard another voice calling, too. It sounded like Pete Saltenstall, our neighbor.

"Pa!" I shouted. "Pa, I'm here!"

"Matt! Matt! Where are you?"

He'd heard! "Here! I'm here!" I cried. I ran blindly through the snow in the direction of Pa's voice, until at last, up ahead, I saw a lantern's pale glow.

"Pa!"

"Matt!" Pa burst out of the snowstorm, caught me up, and hugged me fiercely.

"Lord, boy," he said in a voice choked with worry. "Where'd you get to? You had me scared to death."

"Are you okay?" asked Pete, holding up his lantern to get a good look at me.

"I'm fine," I said. "Just a little cold is all, but Sara's hurt bad. It was a bear, Pa." I blurted out the rest of the story, my words tumbling over each other in my haste to get them said. "We got to get back to Sara quick, Pa," I pleaded at the end. "I don't know how long she can hold out."

Pa nodded. "Do you remember the way?" he asked.

I turned and looked back. The wind and snow were already erasing my tracks. I wasn't sure I'd be able to tell where I'd gone off the trail.

"I don't know," I said. "All I know is, Sara told me to keep the North Star off my left shoulder all the way home."

Pa pulled back and furrowed his brow.

"Who told you?" he asked.

I chewed my lip. "Sara," I said, "or maybe it was Ma. I'm not sure."

Pa and Pete exchanged dubious glances, and I could see what they were thinking.

"I know it sounds crazy," I said. "But it's true. I'm here, aren't I?"

Pa shook his head. "Matt, you're cold and tired," he said. "I think maybe your mind is…"

"No!" I insisted. "My mind is not playing tricks. Sara told me how to get home and I took it on faith, like Ma always said, and I'm here. Now you better take it on faith and believe me 'cause Sara needs help and she needs it fast."

Pa took in a deep breath and blew it out slow, then he lifted his hat and scratched his head.

"You want me to follow the directions a dog gave you?" he asked.

Pete started to laugh. "Well," he said, "come to think of it, I never have known a dog to get lost."

Pa surrendered a smile. "All right, son," he said. "We'll give it a try. We'll take it on faith." He took off his coat and wrapped it around me. "You go on home with Pete now. Your little brother's worried half to death about you."

"No, Pa," I said. "Pete can tell Jamie I'm okay. I got to go with you. I got to get back to Sara."

Pa started to shake his head, but I grabbed his hand in both of mine and squeezed.

"Please, Pa," I begged.

Pa exchanged glances with Pete again, then he looked at me and nodded.

"Let's go," he said.

CHAPTER EIGHT

We followed my tracks as far as we could see them; then Pa pulled out his compass.

"If she said to keep the North Star off your left shoulder," Pa mumbled more to himself than to me, "then we'd need to keep it off our right to get back to her." He took a reading.

"Trail's still heading true," he said.

We followed the logging trail a while longer, with Pa checking his compass every few yards. At last the trail curved left and Pa nodded right.

"Here," he said, and we struck off into the woods. We scrambled down, down the steep bank, slipping and sliding in the snow. When we got to the bottom, Pa checked his compass again and pointed the way.

"She was near a big pine tree," I said.

Pa shone the lantern around every big pine tree we passed. A yellow dog lying still would be easy to miss in the snow.

My heart thumped harder with every step. It was so cold and Sara was hurt so bad. What if...*Don't think that way*, I warned myself. *She promised. You got to have faith.*

"What's that over there?" asked Pa. He lifted the lantern and I peered through the snow to see a still white mound lying just off to the side of a great pine.

"That's her," I whispered, my voice sticking in my throat.

"Sara?" called Pa.

The mound didn't move. I started toward it, but Pa put out a hand to hold me back.

"I think you better let me go first, son," he said.

"No," I said stubbornly. "She's all right. She promised."

I could see the doubt in Pa's eyes and it frightened me.

"She promised!" I cried. "Why don't you believe me?"

Pa stared at me solemnly. "Go ahead, then," he said quietly.

I walked forward on shaky legs, wishing I felt as sure on the inside as my words sounded on the outside. I dropped to my knees beside the mound and brushed the snow from Sara's still face.

"Hey, girl," I said softly.

There was no sign of life. I slid my hand over her side, feeling for the rise and fall of her breathing. I felt only stillness. My heart rose up and thumped in my throat. I bent down and laid my face against her fur.

"Sara. You promised," I whispered. "You promised...."

And then I heard it, ever so softly—the faint bump, bump, bump of her heart.

CHAPTER NINE

Jamie had dragged a chair over to the window and sat watching for us until he'd fallen asleep with his head on the sill. Pete's wife, Mary, fearing to wake him, had tucked a blanket around him right where he sat. He stirred a little when Pa picked him up to carry him to bed.

"Sara," he mumbled.

"She's still alive," I assured him. "We're taking her into town to see Doc Parten."

Jamie nodded, but I'm not sure he even

heard. He was dead asleep again before his head hit the pillow.

"Pete and I'll stay with him," Mary told us. "And we'll tend to your animals if you're not back come morning. You stay as long as need be."

Pa nodded gratefully. Pete had gone to the barn to hitch up our wagon. He drove it around to the front of the house, and Pa carried Sara out. I hopped up in the back and spread out a couple of horse blankets, and Pa laid Sara down gentle beside me. I tucked one of the blankets around her.

"Take care," said Pete as Pa climbed into the driver's seat. "Storm looks to be a fast mover, but it'll be tough going for a while."

"We'll get through," said Pa, then he snapped the reins. "Gee up!" he called to Ned and Bessie, and we moved off into the night.

Doc Parten came to the door scratching himself through his long johns. From the look on his face I guess we were about the last sight he wanted to see on Christmas Eve.

"Dog's been in a tussle with a bear," Pa told him. "She's tore up pretty bad."

Doc didn't say a word. He just carried his lantern around to the back of the wagon and lifted the blanket off of Sara. He started pushing and poking at her. He lifted her chin and looked at her neck. He pulled down her eyelids and looked in her eyes. Then he opened her mouth and pulled out her tongue. She never moved a muscle. Doc sighed and shook his head.

"She's pretty far gone," he said. "Might be kinder just to let her go."

Pa looked at me and tears filled up my

eyes. He put a hand on my shoulder and squeezed.

"My boys've been through a tough spell these past few months, Doc," he said. "I'd be obliged if you could do what you can for the dog."

Doc looked at me, then he nodded slowly.

"You bring her on in, then," he said with a sigh. "But I got to warn you, I'm not promising any miracles."

Doc's office was in a little room in his house.

"You can wait in the parlor," he told us. "Just keep silent and don't wake the house."

Doc's parlor was still and cold, lit only by the dying embers of the evening's fire. Wind whistled down the chimney and rattled at the windowpanes. Pa and I sat silent for a time, me puzzling out the night's events in my head and Pa doing the same, I reckon.

"Pa?" I said at last.

"Yes, son?"

"If animals *were* to talk on Christmas Eve, where do you figure their voices would come from?"

"I don't know," said Pa. "I guess I never gave that much thought."

"Do you think it could be angels talking for them?" I asked.

Pa stared into the embers and considered awhile. "Could be, I s'pose," he said at last. "Your ma always said God had a special love for his dumb critters."

"Ma had a special love for critters, too, didn't she, Pa?"

"Oh, that's for sure," said Pa, smiling sadly. "That's for sure."

"You reckon Ma's an angel, Pa?" I asked.

Pa's eyes grew shiny in the firelight. "I reckon your ma was an angel even before she died, son," he said. "Ain't no doubt about it now."

I sat back in my chair and asked no more. My puzzling was done.

Doc came out at last, wiping his hands on a towel.

"I patched her up," he said. "But she's lost a lot of blood. If she makes it till mornin', she'll probably pull through, but I got to be straight with you. Odds are stacked against it."

I bit my lip and looked at the floor.

"You might as well go on home," said Doc. "There's nothing more anybody can do for her tonight."

I looked up at Pa and shook my head. "Please, no, Pa," I said. "We can't just leave her."

Pa nodded. "We'll stay, if you don't mind," he said to Doc.

"Suit yourself," said Doc. "There's a cot in the office."

Pa and I went into Doc's office and found Sara lying all bandaged up on a blanket in the corner. She was asleep, breathing shallow and fast. Every few seconds her body shuddered.

"You can have the cot," I told Pa. "I want to sleep by Sara."

Pa glanced at me worriedly. "She doesn't look good, Matt," he said.

"She'll be okay," I told him. "Ma'll take care of her."

Pa sighed deeply and laid a hand on my shoulder. "Matt," he said gently. "Faith is a good thing. But it's no guarantee that things are going to go your way."

I swallowed hard and said nothing. Pa took me by the shoulders and turned me to face him square.

"Life isn't always easy, Matt," he said. "We

both know that. But it goes on. You're the one who's shown me that. Whatever the morning brings, I want you to remember, we still got each other—you and me and Jamie—and we'll go on."

I blinked back tears and nodded. "I know, Pa," I said.

Pa pulled me close and gave me a rough hug, then he went over and stretched out on the cot. I lay down next to Sara and rested my hand real gentle on her shoulder. Then I closed my eyes and prayed.

"Please, Ma," I whispered. "I know Pa's saying the truth, and I know we can't always have what we want. But if you got any pull at all up there in heaven, could you help Sara make it to morning? If you can't, I'll understand. But please try, Ma. Please try." Then I fell asleep.

CHAPTER TEN

I awoke in the dim light of dawn to find Pa
leaning over me.

"Well, I'll be…" he whispered softly.

"What?" I asked, rubbing sleep from my
eyes.

"Roll over, Matt," said Pa.

"What?" I repeated.

"Roll over," said Pa.

So I did. And then a warm, wet tongue
licked my face.

•••

It was late morning by the time we got home through the foot of new snow that blanketed the roads. Jamie burst out of the door as soon as we pulled into the yard. He took one look at Sara and started jumping up and down.

"I knew it!" he cried. "I knew she'd be okay."

"And just how did you know that?" asked Pa with a smile as he carried Sara in and laid her down gently on the hearth.

"I prayed all night for Ma to help her," said Jamie. "And then I went out this morning to put the breakfast scraps on the birds' tree and I found this in the branches." He pulled the little dog I had carved for him out from under the Christmas tree and handed it to Pa.

"Ma sent it," he said, his eyes all bright

and glowing. "Ma sent it to tell me that Sara was okay."

Pa took the figure in his hands and stared at it wonderingly. Then he looked over at me.

I smiled.

"It's a miracle, isn't it, Pa?" said Jamie. "Ma sent us a Christmas miracle!"

Pa smiled back at me, then he nodded. "She sure did, Jamie," he said. "She *sure* did."

I knelt beside Sara and stroked her back gently, then I bent down and kissed her head.

"Maybe Ma isn't in the window anymore, Sara," I told her softly. "But I reckon she's still looking out for us."

Author's Note

The Promise is dedicated to and inspired by our own Sara, who has been a part of our family for over twelve years. Sara is a Labrador retriever. As with the Sara in the story, her favorite game is fetching. This is because Labradors were originally bred as bird-hunting dogs and it was their job to retrieve the game that hunters brought down. Because such game often fell into ponds or lakes, Labradors are also strong swimmers. Labradors come in three colors—yellow, black, and chocolate. Sara is a yellow, but she is such a pale yellow that people often mistake her for white.

Labrador retrievers are wonderful family dogs. They are gentle and loving and have a calm, even temperament. They are also extremely bright and sensitive. They can sense when a family member is sad or sick and will shower that person with extra affection. And they will grieve when a loved one dies.

Although usually calm, Labradors, especially

females, can be fiercely aggressive when their homes or families are threatened, taking on larger and stronger animals without hesitation. Although our Sara has never come face to face with a bear (as far as I know), we do have bears in the woods behind our home, and I have always taken great comfort in having her along when I walk there alone.

Sara has never actually spoken to us, but we have often seen "knowing" in her eyes.